GHOST BLADES

If you enjoy reading this book,
you might like to try another story
from the **MAMMOTH READ** series:

Charlie's Champion Chase Hazel Townson
How's Harry? Steve May
Delilah Alone Jenny Nimmo

GHOST BLADES

Anthony Masters
Illustrated by Chris Price

mammoth

First published in Great Britain in 1997 by Mammoth
an imprint of Reed International Books Ltd
Michelin House, 81 Fulham Road, London SW3 6RB
and Auckland, Melbourne, Singapore and Toronto

ISBN 0 7497 2903 1

10 9 8 7 6 5 4 3 2

A CIP catalogue record for this book is
available from the British Library

Printed in Great Britain by Cox & Wyman Ltd,
Reading, Berkshire

For Simon with much love
A.M.

To Delisia
C.P.

One

TERRY SPED DOWN one of the paths in the park, putting in some power-packed turns and a few extra spins as well. He was really getting used to the blades now, feeling more confident, pushing out hard each side and bending forward at the same time.

'Stop!' yelled Alan, the owner of the purple and black Rollerblades. The boys had planned to buy them together, but Terry's dad had been made redundant and he couldn't afford to give him pocket money any more. Alan had been generous though and often let Terry borrow the blades.

'What's up?' Terry bent his left knee and

swung his right foot backwards, digging in his heel and coming to a slightly wobbling stop. He knew he still hadn't got the pressure right and was just about to explain the problem when Alan snapped,

'Come on, hand them over. I want them back.'

'You said I could borrow them any time,' protested Terry.

'Well you can't. Anyway, I've been thinking . . .' he stumbled. 'I should have asked for them back last week.'

'Why last week?'

'Because I said.'

Alan looked uneasy.

'It's not fair,' Terry stared at him, more amazed than annoyed. 'What's happened?'

'Nothing's happened. I've just changed my mind – that's all.'

'You mean I can't borrow them any more?' Terry was getting angry now.

'I'm going to sell them to buy a
fishing-rod.'

'You don't like fishing,' Terry told him.

'I do now,' Alan replied stubbornly, and
Terry knew he meant business. 'Now give
me my blades.'

Snapping open the clasps, Terry unlaced the boots and practically threw them at him.

'I'm sorry . . .' Now Alan had got them back he wanted to be friendly again.

'Yeah.' Terry was in a deep sulk and he wasn't likely to come out of it for a long time.

'I'll lend you my rod.'

'I don't want your rod,' yelled Terry. 'I'll never want your stupid rod. And you're not telling me the truth, are you? I bet you're going to share those blades with someone else.' Terry ran off before Alan could see the tears in his eyes.

That night, Terry could think of nothing but the blades. Miserably he imagined Alan sharing them with someone else. He kept seeing another boy riding them – someone who was much better than him, someone who had become Alan's best friend.

Terry was small for his age, with blond hair and blue eyes. He hated the way he looked. He wanted to be tall and athletic like Alan. The blades had made a big difference to Terry. He wasn't much good at sport, too small for basketball and not fast enough for football and rugby. He hated cricket and didn't like swimming because he had an allergy to chlorine. The blades though – they were different. He could really be somebody on those and he was sure he was becoming more skilful. But now his blading days were over.

Two

TERRY GOT UP next morning in a very bad mood, but at least he had a plan.

His parents and his little sister were already sitting round the breakfast table when he came downstairs.

'You're late,' said Lucy. 'And you haven't combed your hair.'

Grimly, Terry realised she was out to get him for spraying her with a water-pistol the previous night. He had wanted to take it out on someone – and Lucy had been a walking target.

'Shut up, you,' he muttered.

'Don't speak to your sister like that,' said Dad, gloomily scanning the Situations

Vacant section of the local paper.

Terry realised he hadn't made a good start. 'Sorry.'

'Sorry to who?' Lucy was triumphant.

'Sorry, Lucy.'

'You ought to say that on your knees,' she said. 'You soaked my pyjamas . . . '

'I've said sorry.' Terry gave her an almost pleading look but she stuck out her tongue at him. He turned to his father. 'Dad. Can you do me a favour?'

'Depends what it is.'

'Alan's going to sell his Rollerblades.'

'Is he now?'

'To buy a rod. Or that's what he says.'

Slowly his father lowered the paper. There was genuine concern in his eyes. 'I can't do it, Tel. I can barely cope with the bills I've got. He paused. 'I would if I could. You know that.'

'I know that,' muttered Terry, realising

how stupid he'd been.

'I'm sorry.' His father's voice shook slightly. Mum looked away and for once Lucy had nothing to say.

Later, Terry cycled past Alan's house, trying to think how he could make him change his mind. In the end, he decided the only way was to talk to him again and make him see sense – or at least his point of view.

He went in the back way to avoid Alan's mum, but directly he got to the door she was there, grinning, her hands on her hips. It was as if she had sensed him coming and was lying in wait.

'Well, if it isn't my Terry.'

'Is Alan in?' he asked hesitantly.

'He's got a terrible cold, sneezing everywhere. I wouldn't go up – you don't want to catch it.'

To his great annoyance, she gently patted his head.

'OK. See you.' Terry ducked under her arm and ran towards the gate. As he passed the shed he hesitated, knowing that was where Alan kept the blades. Were they still there? Or had he already sold them?

Terry tiptoed through the open door. The blades gleamed in the darkness so temptingly he could hardly bear to look at them. Why couldn't he have a last go? As Alan was ill he couldn't use them and he wouldn't be selling them either. Not yet.

They were just sitting there, waiting. No one would mind. Not if he brought them back by lunchtime. Or even just before bedtime. Slowly, Terry tried to convince himself that borrowing wasn't stealing.

Rain began to spatter on the tin roof of the shed but that didn't worry him. What was a bit of rain if he had the blades? He could put in hours of practice and Alan wouldn't even know, not if he got them back without being seen. Anyway, it wasn't stealing. Before he'd decided to sell them, Alan had said he could share them, use the blades any time.

Three

ONCE HE WAS speeding down the hill, Terry's guilt vanished. All he could feel was the drizzle on his face and the wonderful freedom in his feet as he twisted and turned, skimming his way along the shining wet pavements.

Now he was darting his way through the town, the blades so light that at times he almost seemed to be flying. Terry felt terrific, but knew he was still in control, going as fast as he dared.

Twenty minutes later, Terry was blading through the run-down streets at the other end of town. The clouds scudding overhead were black now and the drizzle had changed to spitting rain. Closed-up

shops, boarded buildings, rows of empty houses stretched around him and a large sign read:

LONGSIDE DEVELOPMENT
BEGINS SPRING

Terry passed yet another derelict building, this time much more distinctive than the others. Set back behind a crumbling stone wall, it was high, with attic rooms in the eaves that looked like staring eyes. Glancing up, for a second Terry thought he saw a boy's face at the window. Then it disappeared and he put it down to his imagination.

He swooped on down the street, gathering speed again and letting out a whoop of joy. Then the blades suddenly turned round in a small circle and carried him back the way he had come. The shock was so great that Terry felt completely numb. It was unbelievable – but the blades had taken control. How could that possibly happen?

Faster and faster the blades carried Terry along the pavement, weaving their way in and out of startled pedestrians. Terry's throat was dry and he could feel his heart thumping as if it were trying to get out of his chest. He tried to stop, but the blades didn't respond. The force that was pulling

him could not be broken.

The tall house loomed above him; dark, low cloud swirling around its roof. Large black streaks covered the walls and the windows were boarded up. The only exception was one of the attic rooms. Wasn't that where he had seen the face of the boy?

But there was no time to think. He was far too scared and the blades seemed to be going even faster now.

Suddenly Terry found himself skidding round the corner of the house, hurtling down a narrow path through long wet grass. Taking the next corner at an incredible speed, sure that at any moment he was going to fall, the blades turned him at an alarming angle towards the back garden gate.

Terry watched the scarred mossy wood rush towards him and tried to brace himself, his mouth open in a silent scream. The blades were being propelled by such an incredibly strong force that however hard he pressed down on his right heel to try and brake them, they refused to respond.

Then the gate flew open.

Terry jarred his shoulder as he clipped the post, speeding along a path that was overgrown with stinging nettles. They lashed at his arms as he ploughed through, but still the blades weren't slowing down.

The garden was becoming a blur, and he bounced over a plank of wood that was burnt and cracked, almost losing his balance. Desperately he righted himself and rounded an old greenhouse. He saw that he was heading straight for the back door.

Soon he was so close that he could see every detail of the big rusty lock and burnt green paint. Then, just as he was about to make impact, the door abruptly swung open. To his horror he was propelled inside a dark and misty smelling room.

The blades shuddered to a halt and the door slammed shut behind him.

Pulling off the blades, Terry ran back to

the door and tried to open it, but it was stuck. He rattled and pushed and shoved and pulled but it wouldn't budge, and for some time he battered at the heavy wood in terrible panic. Had the door jammed? Locked itself? He couldn't remember seeing a key.

As a last effort he threw himself against the door, jarring his already bruised shoulder. But it was no good. He was trapped.

Miserably, Terry gazed around the room. It was a kitchen containing a few badly burnt bits of furniture – a table, some chairs, a couple of wall cupboards, a partly broken mirror and a singed calendar with a picture of a large house, its smooth lawns running down to a lake.

The walls were black and peeling and the ceiling was bubbled and scarred. The calendar was headed:

English Country Homes and Gardens
1965

All the scorched surfaces in the room were covered with a thick coating of dust, which had clearly not been disturbed for a long time. Terry shivered. The place seemed to have an expectant air, giving him the uncanny impression that it was waiting for something. For him? He shrugged off this notion, knowing his imagination was running away with him.

Two windows were boarded up and the other, although broken, was too small even for Terry to get through. He clambered up on the blackened enamel sink and wrenched at the heavy boards, but they had been nailed tight to keep vandals out.

As he struggled, something soft and silky landed on his neck. It made him jump and he brushed away a spider, which ran over the grimy linoleum, scurrying for cover under the table.

He climbed down, panic surging. Unless someone came he could be here for a long time. But why should anyone come? There had obviously been a fire and the house had been left derelict for years. He thought of his parents and Lucy, and felt the helpless tears pricking at the backs of his eyelids.

Four

THE RAIN BEGAN again, pelting on to the roof, and Terry saw a steady trickle sliding down the opposite wall. He knew there was no point in just standing around, accepting he was inexplicably trapped and doing nothing about it. He would have to force himself to penetrate the darkness and explore the rest of the house.

Terry pulled open the door and gazed into a hallway. A pool of grey light filtered down from a hole in the ceiling. There was a table with a vase of dusty dried flowers, and a tattered picture of a family. Mother and father, a boy of about his own age and an older girl all sat in deckchairs on a newly

mown lawn. Terry picked it up and looked
at it intently; the girl's face was vaguely
familiar. But why should the photograph
have been left here? The house looked as if
it had been empty for a long time. He
shivered, feeling so tense he could hardly
breathe.

There was a mass of faded circulars scattered on the mat and a strong cindery smell in the air. Then he saw the blisters on the paintwork, the great swathe of scorch-marks on the wallpaper. Suddenly he was afraid, very afraid.

He hurried to the front door and tried to open it, but he should have known there would be no easy way out. Again and again he tried to free the lock, but it was hopeless.

He ran into the sitting room, which was completely empty, its windows boarded up, and then into the dining room.

He was sure he had heard something. Something upstairs. A rat? A footstep? But he could hear nothing now – and the silence seemed to go on for a very long time, like a dense blanket around him. Then he heard it again; a distinct, slightly creaking tread as if someone was moving slowly, watching him from the landing, waiting to come down.

Terry stared up the blackened staircase.

Was that a shadow? A movement? A shape?

Then he heard more footsteps, light as the rain but quite unmistakeable; footsteps that were even now stealing down the stairs.

To begin with Terry couldn't see anyone; he was shivering so hard that the staircase seemed blurred. His heart pounded fiercely, sweat ran into his eyes, his mouth was so dry that he knew he couldn't speak. Dry as cinders. Dry as the fire-damaged house.

Then the boy appeared.

At first he was insubstantial, but then his outline became much stronger and Terry could see he was wearing a short-sleeved white shirt, grey shorts, long socks and sandals. The boy's expression was blank and his face was incredibly white. His hair was cut very short.

Suddenly the blankness was replaced by mocking eyes, a grinning mouth, a look of pleasure and of triumph.

'Got you,' he said.

'Who are you?' rasped Terry.

'Joe.' The boy spoke in a whisper. 'I've no one to play with.' He paused. 'There was another boy. He was on those skate things. But he went away. Then I saw you.'

'You made me come here,' stuttered Terry. 'You turned the blades round. How?'

'That would be telling.' The boy's grin widened.

'I want to go home.' Terry couldn't move; it was as if he was a heavy stone statue, and a picture of playing statues years ago at a birthday party flashed into his mind. 'You can't move,' his friend's mother had said. 'No one can move. You're all made of stone.'

Joe came nearer, smelling cold and earthy. 'I've been trying hard recently – trying hard to make friends.'

'I want to go home,' repeated Terry.

'You can't,' said Joe. 'You're my friend now. You have to do what I tell you.'

Terry could feel a tightness in his stomach and his legs were leaden, but with an enormous effort he broke away from Joe

and ran to the front door, pulling and shaking and rattling with all his strength. But it still wouldn't move.

Joe laughed.

'Let me go,' yelled Terry.

'I'll never do that,' he said quietly.

Terry felt the power of the boy in his mind, knowing instinctively how strong he was, how difficult it was going to be to get away. Whatever he did he couldn't seem to escape from the house. Could he try to talk his way out instead? Convince this boy that he had to let him go, that he had no right to trap him?

'Do you live here?' he asked, playing for time, knowing that something was wrong with Joe, horribly wrong. There was a strange shimmering around the boy's shoulders, as if they weren't quite formed.

'Have you seen my sister?' he asked. The triumphant smile had vanished. 'She's older than me. She'll know where my parents are. She looks after me.'

'I haven't seen anyone.'

Joe looked at him threateningly, his misty features twisted in anger. 'I can't find her.' There was an awkward pause and then he said abruptly, as if he was deliberately changing his mood, 'Come up and play.'

The invitation was the most threatening Terry had ever received. He didn't want to go upstairs and play. Not with Joe.

'They've gone and left me alone. It's not fair.'

Terry remembered the old photograph. 'What's your sister's name?'

'Liz.'

There was another long silence between them and Terry was swept with despair. He didn't understand what was going on. He didn't want to understand.

'I'm sorry,' he said at last. 'I've got to go

home now. Can you let me out?' Terry was trying to be reasonable, trying to talk himself out of a nightmare.

Joe clenched his fists. The dank earthy smell was more intense. 'You don't like me, do you? I fight people if they don't like me.'

'I just want to go home. What's so bad about that? You forced me to come here.'

His pale features twisted in rage, Joe hit out, but his fist went straight through Terry's chest and all he could feel was a blast of cold air that chilled him to the bone.

'You're a ghost,' he stuttered un-believingly. 'A ghost.'

'Don't be stupid,' said Joe. 'Ghosts don't exist. I've never believed in them. My mum told me not to. Didn't yours?'

Terry couldn't think what to reply. Then he noticed, with a sudden shock, that the stairs had changed. They had become soft and pliable, as if they were made of silk, and they shimmered just as Joe's shoulders did. The sight was horrifying and the sweat from his forehead poured into his eyes. Was this really happening to him or was he ill?

'We could play football,' Joe wheedled.

'Upstairs?'

'You can do anything upstairs.'

Desperately, Terry tried another tack. 'Let's go outside.' He had to get away from those silky stairs.

Joe gazed at him perplexed. 'I can't go outside.'

'Why not?'

'I can't. You come with me.' He was getting angry all over again.

Terry grabbed the blades. He felt beaten, tearful, and he didn't know what to do next. Joe was walking towards him.

'I don't want to,' said Terry stubbornly. 'I'm not going upstairs.'

'I'll make you.' Joe smirked, knowing his power.

'If you come outside,' said Terry, trying to ignore the threat, determined not to give in, 'you can have a go on my Rollerblades.'

'You mean roller-skates?'

'Sort of.'

'I've got mine upstairs.' Once again he used that terrifying word. 'You can see them in my room.'

But Terry was still determined that he wouldn't go up those silky stairs. They seemed to be rustling slightly now, as if they were waves lapping gently on a shore. Instead, he suddenly dashed back into the kitchen and threw himself against the door.

But yet again, nothing happened. Joe giggled. It was a sinister sound.

'They're nice,' he said, but didn't attempt to touch them. 'Better than roller-skates.'

'No one uses roller-skates now.'

Once again Joe was puzzled. 'But mine are new. Mum's only just bought them. I'll show you.'

'No.'

'I told you – I'll make you.'

'You won't!'

Joe grinned. 'Just see.' He stepped back, staring, a malicious smile on his chalk white face. Terry felt a tight band round his mind. He knew he would do just what Joe said. He had to do what Joe said.

Like a robot he walked towards the stairs while Joe turned his shimmering back on him and began to run up. Terry followed shakily, feeling as if he was treading on soggy cotton-wool that would give way at any minute. He could smell cold earth again.

Five

WHEN TERRY REACHED the landing, he gasped in disbelief. He had expected to see a burnt-out ruin, but instead he was standing on an unmarked linoleum. In front of him each door had a plaque. *MUM & DAD. ELIZABETH. JOE.*

There were pictures on the shining white walls, a table scattered with magazines and a vase of fresh flowers. It was as if the house was lived in again – as if the fire hadn't happened.

Joe pushed open his bedroom door and ran inside. As Terry followed him, he saw the shimmering again, on the edges of the wall, on the pictures, the table, even on a pair of football boots. He touched the door

and it was like the stairs – soft and silky, slightly moist.

Joe's bedroom was hazy. It was also an incredible mess; the bed was unmade, half buried under a mound of comics, and the floor was covered with toys – miniature cars on a race track, a football, a train set, a cricket bat and stumps and a half-finished jigsaw puzzle. Football posters were plastered over most of the walls and a dartboard hung askew.

Terry gazed into Joe's face, half recognising something familiar, just like he had with the girl in the photograph downstairs.

'Why are you staring at me?'

'You remind me of someone.'

'Who?'

Then the memory clicked. Joe reminded him of Alan.

'I can't remember,' he hedged, not

wanting any more complications, still trying to focus his mind on how to escape.

'Thanks a lot.'

Joe went over to his roller-skates and began to put them on, reminding Terry that he was still clutching the precious blades.

'Let's go then,' he said calmly.

'Outside?' The relief was so great that Terry felt an overwhelming sense of release.

'No. Just get your blades on!' The threat was back and slowly, reluctantly, Terry did as he was told.

'Now,' said Joe, gazing ahead. As his eyes widened, so did the walls, until he and Terry were standing in a cold, blank space that seemed to stretch to infinity.

'What's happening?' Terry gasped, his panic increasing.

'It won't last long. Do you know what? I saw Mum and Dad walking on the horizon out there the other day. I couldn't get to them though. It wasn't fair.' There was a catch in Joe's voice. 'But ever since I saw them I got strong. I got strong enough to make friends.'

Take prisoners, more likely, thought Terry.

'Let's get going,' said Joe. 'Before the space closes down.'

His heart pounding, Terry started to rollerblade while Joe skated. At first he was cautious, waiting for the walls to reappear, but as Joe began to speed up so did he, and soon they were both hurtling along what appeared to be smooth, bare wooden boards that stretched limitlessly in front of them.

An unexpected feeling of sudden joy filled Terry and his fear temporarily disappeared. Joe was beside him, but he was just a blur, and the sensation of speed increased as they both flew on to nowhere. Terry had never felt such a glorious sense of freedom before, never felt such happiness. It was extraordinary.

Above them, slowly emerging from a bank of low, foggy cloud, was a vast canopy of stars, their light bright and piercing, icy cold.

Soon Terry was no longer cautious and was blading faster and faster, staring up at the heavens above, with all their jewelled clarity. He could see the constellations, the Milky Way, and a huge white moon that had its own special radiance.

Terry's spirits lifted until he was so elated he was yelling in delight.

Then, with a snap, the space closed

down and he hit the wall.

Terry saw stars again, but this time in his head. Slowly the pain went, leaving him dizzy and sick, and he began to tremble with shock and despair. He wanted the space again, wanted to feel the heady delight, but instead he was back in the misty misery of Joe's ghostly bedroom.

Joe was sitting on the floor, quietly undoing his skates as if nothing had happened. Terry refocused abruptly, taking off his blades, knowing he was trapped again.

'I'm always stuck in this house,' complained Joe. 'Sometimes the space comes when I put on my roller-skates. Most times it doesn't.'

'What is the space?' asked Terry in bewilderment.

'I don't know. Once I thought it was

heaven. But it's always closing down. It's not fair. My sister wouldn't let me be unhappy like this. She's older than me.' He paused. 'I'm waiting for her to tell me what to do.' Joe was glaring at Terry with growing hostility. 'It's all right for you, isn't it? You're free.' Then he grinned but the grin was malicious again. 'Or at least you think you are.'

'What are you on about?' demanded Terry.

'If you don't tell me where my family is, I'll keep you here for ever. If Liz won't help me – you will!'

A cold, clammy hand seemed to be creeping about in Terry's stomach. 'You can't do that.'

'Want me to show you what I can do?' Joe got up and began to walk towards him.

'There's nothing you can do to me.' Terry tried bravado.

'So how do you think you got here?'

'On my blades.'

'Just like that?'

It wasn't just like that, but Terry wasn't going to admit anything. He was locked in battle with Joe, and although he wasn't sure if he could win he knew he had to try. He couldn't give up and become his prisoner.

'I made your blades come,' said Joe calmly, as if it was all quite natural.

'I'm going home,' Terry replied shakily. As he spoke he wondered if he should tell Joe that he looked a bit like Alan. Would that make any difference? Would that make Joe help him? But perhaps it wasn't such a good idea. If he did tell him, then Joe might drag Alan into all this too. Terry couldn't let him do that, so he had to use his willpower instead. 'Goodbye, Joe,' he said firmly. 'I'm going now.'

The football began to bounce on its own, slowly at first and then speeding up, getting higher and higher. The noise in the quiet hazy room seemed incredibly loud.

Grabbing the blades Terry ran to the door, and when he glanced back, saw to his amazement that the attic room was empty. It had charred walls and a blackened ceiling. There was no bed, no scattering of possessions, no Joe. Only the football that was bouncing along beside him.

What kind of trick was this, Terry wondered, reaching for the handle. Was Joe letting him go? Just like that? After all his threats? It didn't seem likely. And yet . . .

He pulled open the door and the football hit him on the head – hard. The ball hit him again and again, with such ferocity that Terry lashed out, trying to drive it away. But the football kept bouncing between him and the dangerously crumbling stairs, herding Terry back into Joe's room.

He collapsed on the floor, still fighting the football as it bounced off his doubled-

up body, hitting his face and shoulders, the leather stinging painfully, until Terry yelled, 'Stop it, Joe. You've got to stop.'

But the football went on punishing him to the sound of Joe's delighted laughter.

Six

SLOWLY THE BEDROOM reformed itself. Joe sat grinning on his rumpled comic-strewn bed, still laughing in his awful muddle of a prison. The football bounced itself back into a corner, while Terry clambered to his feet, bruised and shaken.

'I can make that ball do things,' said Joe. 'It's my weapon. Useful, isn't it? I can do other things too,' he added, but now his eyes were full of tears. 'I can see the past. Or some of it. But it frightens me, and afterwards – when I've looked back – I get really tired and I have to rest for a while.' Joe paused. 'Something happened,' he said. 'Something frightening, but I don't fully understand what.' He paused and looked more hopeful. 'Maybe *you* will.' He closed his eyes and the room moved with a life of its own, shifting restlessly like an ocean. A cold wind sent the football rolling across the floor and Joe and the mess in his bedroom began to shimmer.

Clothes drifted back into cupboards, the bed made itself, the mountain of comics rose in the air and sorted themselves into a tidy pile on the floor. The miniature cars and race track flew on to the shelf, the half-finished jigsaw took itself to pieces and drifted into a chest, closely followed by the cricket ball and stumps. The darts board straightened itself up and Joe got into bed. He slept.

Then Terry watched the bedroom door slowly open.

A middle-aged woman quietly came in and went over to Joe. Although her clothes were out-dated she was beautiful, tall and elegant, wearing a long dress. A man in a dark suit quietly followed.

Joe's mother put a finger to her lips and leant over her son, kissing his cheek.

'God bless,' she said. 'Sleep tight.'

'Don't forget to leave the light on, Mum,'

he muttered, waking but still half asleep.

'Of course I won't. Do I ever?'

His parents crept out, gently closed the door and Joe turned over, snuggling down again.

Terry didn't want to watch any more because he was sure something dreadful was going to happen. This was much worse than the ghostly bullying, but he had to stay now, had to be with Joe while the terrible thing happened.

Thunder began to grumble outside and lightning flashed. Terry could dimly hear the murmur of voices downstairs and the radio was playing a song he recognised:

Smile when you feel like crying,
Laugh when you feel like dying . . .

Never had Joe's room seemed so terrifying, but Terry knew he had to be beside him, knew he had to understand.

Thunder growled again but Joe slept on. The room was almost completely silent except for the distant sounds of life downstairs.

Then suddenly the plug in the wall socket began to crackle, throwing out sparks and then little darts of blue flame. To Terry's horror, the darts became tongues, leaping at the carpet with a little spluttering sound. Slowly the material ignited and dense black smoke billowed towards Joe's bed.

Terry wanted to wake him, to stop it all happening, but he knew he couldn't. This was the past. It couldn't be altered.

Joe began to cry out and Terry was again desperate to help him. He wanted to warn Joe, to drag him from the bed, but it was as if his legs were encased in concrete. The smoke covered the bed like a dark blanket and Joe began to choke. Then the door burst open and his parents ran in, disbelief in their eyes, their faces deeply shocked.

As if sensing more victims, the smoke leapt towards them, a great black spume of death.

Suddenly, the terrible scene seemed to snap shut, as if a blind had come down, and Terry was plunged back into darkness.

54

Then it gradually lifted and he realised he was in the middle of the burnt-out room. The only object that remained was the football, which was motionless.

What about Joe's sister, Terry wondered. Had Elizabeth died in the fire too? And why did Joe remind him so much of Alan?

'Joe,' he whispered.

There was no reply. Terry heard the traffic rumbling outside and wondered if he could escape at last. But what about the burnt stairs? Would he be able to climb down?

'Joe?'

Slowly a little mist rose from the blackened floor and he could see him, barely formed, just a thin sliver of a boy. As Joe had predicted, he was totally exhausted by bringing back his terrible past.

Terry hurried to the door, opened it and then paused. No football bounced at him. No unseen power pulled him back. Was Joe so tired he couldn't hold him here any longer, or would he regain his strength and his power over him?

In the end Terry realised he was in control again. Joe had lost out because he had tried to show him the past, in the hope he could be helped. Terry paused. Joe had gambled and lost. Surely he owed him something. Surely he couldn't just leave him here alone. For ever. 'I'll try to find them,' he muttered over his shoulder. 'I promise I will.'

But when Terry arrived at the top of the stairs, he realised that escape wasn't going to be easy, for they were no longer silky smooth. The stairs were almost burnt through.

Slowly he began to edge his way down, stepping as gingerly as possible, sure the charred stair treads would crumble at any moment. He felt something give and tried to step back, but his foot plunged through the burnt-out stair.

Trapped in carbonised wood that he knew might give way at any moment, Terry stared down into the dark abyss below. He was alone. Just like Joe.

'Joe!' Terry yelled desperately, trying not to move.

There was no response, only a deep, impenetrable silence.

'I need you, Joe,' he whispered. 'I need you.'

Still no reply.

'Please, Joe. Please.'

The whispering slowly began, penetrating the burnt shell of the building, seeming to come from everywhere, rising and falling on the dead air of the abandoned house.

'Too weak. Too weak.'

'Joe!' Terry moved slightly and then gave an agonised yell as the stairs began to crumble. A large section fell into the stairwell with a loud thud and Terry wondered if he would soon plunge after it. Then he and Joe would be ghosts together, companions for ever with only the space – that mysterious space – to give them a brief glimpse of freedom. But that wouldn't be enough. Would never be enough.

As the knocking on the front door began, the freezing cold earthy smell returned and the stairs jerked into their silky texture again.

'Go now,' whispered Joe. 'I can't hold on.'

Without hesitation Terry desperately worked his way carefully down the two flights of stairs, the Rollerblades still tightly gripped in his hand. He could see the front door being rattled, and as it slowly and unwillingly opened, the silky stairs vanished and Terry was pitched on to the hall floor in a cloud of choking black dust.

Seven

'ARE YOU OK?' Terry dragged himself to his feet, hardly able to believe Alan was standing over him, looking so anxious and questioning.

'I guessed you'd be here when I saw the blades were missing. We came straight down.' Alan stared at Terry incredulously. 'What on earth's been going on?'

'You certainly look a sight.' Mrs Forester tried to stay calm as she stroked his hair in the way he hated. She looked terribly afraid, but there was something else – a deep sadness that her husband seemed to share.

'Are you – Joe's parents?' Terry blurted out.

Mrs Forester shook her head, but before
she could speak, Alan interrupted, the
words tumbling out as if he was glad to
make his confession at last.

'Those blades – they made me come here. I was scared stiff. That's why I wanted to sell them. That's why I didn't want you to have them. But I should have told you.' His voice petered out.

'I'm Joe's sister,' said Mrs Forester slowly and painfully. 'Liz. I never spoke out either – never told Alan about any of this. I couldn't bear to. The house was bought by a property company that went bankrupt.' Her voice broke. 'That's why it was never pulled down. I always wanted to come back, but I never had the courage. I even left that photograph here.' Liz went over and picked it up, staring down, her lips working but no sound coming out.

'What happened, Mum?' asked Alan, running over and putting his arms round her. 'I know my grandparents and my Uncle Joe were killed – but you never said how.'

'We'll talk about it all later,' said his father nervously, as if he were anxious to normalise everything. But Terry knew he couldn't do that.

'Joe's here,' Terry blurted out. 'He's waiting for you.' He gazed up into Liz's horrified eyes.

'What on earth are you talking about?' demanded Mr Forester. 'What is all this nonsense?'

'But no one replied.

'You don't believe in ghosts, do you?' Alan turned to his mother in bewilderment.

'The fire brigade got me out,' Liz said, avoiding the question. 'But Mum and Dad and Joe . . . they all . . . they all died.' Her voice broke and tears flooded down her cheeks.

Then Terry heard footsteps, slowly treading across the burnt floorboards.

Joe stood on the landing, a dim, spectral shape, watching them apprehensively.

'Liz?' It was only the faintest whisper. 'Is that you?'

Liz could hardly bring out the words. 'Yes. It's me. I'm sorry. I'm sorry I let you down so badly, Joe.'

'I knew you'd come,' he said. 'I knew you'd come back.'

Liz held out her trembling arms to him. 'Joe. I love you, Joe. You know I've always loved you. I just couldn't . . . ' Liz smiled up at him through her tears and Terry saw Joe begin to run down the stairs towards his sister. But before he reached her he vanished.

They stood silently for a while. There seemed nothing more to say.

'Some kind of optical illusion,' muttered Mr Forester eventually.

'When they get round to pulling this place down,' said Terry, 'there's a football in Joe's room. You might want to keep it.'

Liz nodded.

'It's disgraceful the way this place has

been left to rot,' continued her husband, determined to ignore the inexplicable. 'I'm going to speak to the council. The building's dangerous. A child might get in . . .' He gazed at Terry and paused, looking embarrassed.

'A child was here all the time,' whispered Liz, 'where I left him.'

'I'm sorry I pinched your blades,' Terry said as he and Alan walked out into the wet street. To Terry the sudden normality seemed as miraculous as the appearance of the never-ending room that he and Joe had skated through earlier.

'I should have told you what happened to me. I could have prevented all this. I'm sorry.' Alan was as bewildered as his father. Neither of them had been able to rationalise the situation. 'I can't believe it. Were you locked in here all the time with Joe's ghost?'

He laughed unhappily.

'Yes,' said Terry. 'But he's gone now. Seeing your mother has set him free.'

Alan looked at him warily and then hurriedly changed the subject. 'We'll share the blades again.' He paused. 'If you think they're safe, I mean.'

'They're safe,' replied Terry quietly.

'We're going back in the car. I feel so lousy with this cold.' Alan took a last look at the sinister shell of a building and shuddered. 'You'd better get in – I'm sure you want to get away from here. I do.'

'I'd rather blade back,' said Terry. 'Tell Mum I'm on my way.'

As he sped through the streets, the rain came down again, soaking him, but Terry didn't mind. He knew the blades would never go as fast now – not without Joe.

Suddenly he realised that, in a strange way, he missed him.

Approaching home, the blades began to speed up, and once again Terry was dangerously out of control. His heart

began to pound and his panic rose until he was dry-mouthed and shaking. It can't be happening again, he thought desperately. It just can't.

Then all at once the blades slowed down, so that he almost fell off.

Could he hear laughter in the wind?

Terry gazed up at the huge open space of the sky. 'Goodbye,' he muttered.

'Goodbye, Joe.'

If you enjoyed this
MAMMOTH READ try:

Charlie's Champion Chase

Hazel Townson
Illustrated by *Philippe Dupasquier*

Charlie goes carol-singing to earn
money for Christmas, although he
knows his mother disapproves. On his
way he stumbles upon a burglary and
kidnapping. Charlie finds a vital clue,
but will anyone take him seriously?
The chase is on, but only Charlie
can avert disaster . . .

Another gripping adventure following
the success of *Charlie the Champion Liar*
and *Charlie the Champion Traveller*.

If you enjoyed this
M<small>AMMOTH</small> R<small>EAD</small> try:

How's Harry?

Steve May
Illustrated by *Philip Hopman*

Harry's a hamster and Kate's going to
have him for a pet, whatever her parents
say. Her dad doesn't think she can look
after him properly – every five minutes
he asks, 'How's Harry?'

It drives Kate mad. All she wants
is to help Harry find happiness. But
when she asks Harry what he wants
from life, he can't tell her.

Kate decides she knows best.
She will take Harry back to his
roots . . . in the Syrian desert!

A Selected List of Fiction from Mammoth

While every effort is made to keep prices low, it is sometimes necessary to increase prices at short notice Mandarin Paperbacks reserves the right to show new retail prices on covers which may differ from those previously advertised in the text or elsewhere.

The prices shown below were correct at the time of going to press.

☐	7497 1421 2	**Betsey Bigalow is Here!**	Malorie Blackman	£2.99
☐	7497 0366 0	**Dilly The Dinosaur**	Tony Bradman	£3.50
☐	7497 0137 4	**Flat Stanley**	Jeff Brown	£3.50
☐	7497 2200 2	**Crazy Shoe Shuffle**	Gillian Cross	£3.99
☐	7497 0592 2	**The Peacock Garden**	Anita Desai	£3.50
☐	7497 1822 6	**Tilly Mint Tales**	Berlie Doherty	£3.50
☑	7497 0054 8	**My Naughty Little Sister**	Dorothy Edwards	£3.50
☐	7497 0723 2	**The Little Prince (colour ed.)**	A. Saint-Exupery	£4.50
☑	7497 0305 9	**Bill's New Frock**	Anne Fine	£3.50
☑	7497 1718 1	**My Grandmother's Stories**	Adèle Geras	£3.50
☐	7497 2611 3	**A Horse for Mary Beth**	Alison Hart	£3.50
☑	7497 1930 3	**The Jessame Stories**	Julia Jarman	£3.50
☑	7497 0420 9	**I Don't Want To**	Bel Mooney	£3.50
☑	7497 0048 3	**Friends and Brothers**	Dick King Smith	£3.50
☑	7497 2596 6	**Billy Rubbish**	Alexander McCall Smith	£3.50
☑	7497 0795 X	**Owl Who Was Afraid of the Dark**	Jill Tomlinson	£3.99

All these books are available at your bookshop or newsagent, or can be ordered direct from the address below. Just tick the titles you want and fill in the form below.

Cash Sales Department, PO Box 5, Rushden, Northants NN10 6YX.
Fax: 01933 414047 : Phone: 01933 414000.

Please send cheque, payable to 'Reed Book Services Ltd.', or postal order for purchase price quoted and allow the following for postage and packing:

£1.00 for the first book, 50p for the second; **FREE POSTAGE AND PACKING FOR THREE BOOKS OR MORE PER ORDER.**

NAME (Block letters)......GARY Booth...

ADDRESS......STRATHEAD FARM (SITE)..................................

......HATTON PETERHEAD AB42 OTA.......................

☐ I enclose my remittance for............................

☐ I wish to pay by Access/Visa Card Number

Expiry Date

Signature . . . .

Please quote our reference: MAND